CAMP CAN'T

by Diana G. Gallagher

illustrated by Brann Garvey

Librarian Reviewer
Laurie K. Holland
Media Specialist (National Board Certified), Edina, MN
MA in Elementary Education, Minnesota State University, Mankato

Reading Consultant
Elizabeth Stedem
Educator/Consultant, Colorado Springs, CO
MA in Elementary Education, University of Denver, CO

STONE ARCH BOOKS
MINNEAPOLIS   SAN DIEGO

Claudia Cristina Cortez is published by Stone Arch Books
151 Good Counsel Drive, P.O. Box 669
Mankato, Minnesota 56002
www.stonearchbooks.com

Library of Congress Cataloging-in-Publication Data
Gallagher, Diana G.
   Camp Can't: The Complicated Life of Claudia Cristina Cortez / by Diana
G. Gallagher; illustrated by Brann Garvey.
   p. cm. — (Claudia Cristina Cortez)
   Summary: Thirteen-year-old Claudia wants to prove that she should be
a junior counselor at Blue River Camp next year, but first she must face mean
girls, the boy she has a crush on, a seven-year-old rascal she often babysits, her
own bad luck, and a challenging swimming test.
   ISBN-13: 978-1-59889-840-8 (library binding)
   ISBN-10: 1-59889-840-X (library binding)
   ISBN-13: 978-1-59889-878-1 (paperback)
   ISBN-10: 1-59889-878-7 (paperback)
   [1. Camps—Fiction. 2. Interpersonal relations—Fiction.
3. Self-realization—Fiction.] I. Garvey, Brann, ill. II. Title.
III. Title: Camp Cannot.
PZ7.G13543Cam 2008
[Fic]—dc22   2007005952

Art Director: Heather Kindseth
Graphic Designer: Kay Fraser

Photo Credits
Delaney Photography, cover

1 2 3 4 5 6 11 10 09 08 07 06

Table of Contents

Cast of

CLAUDIA

That's me. I'm thirteen, and I'm in the seventh grade at Pine Tree Middle School. I live with my mom, my dad, and my brother, Jimmy. I have one cat, Ping-Ping. I like music, baseball, and hanging out with my friends.

MONICA is my very best friend. We met when we were really little, and we've been best friends ever since. I don't know what I'd do without her! Monica loves horses. In fact, when she grows up, she wants to be an Olympic rider!

BECCA is one of my closest friends. She lives next door to Monica. Becca is really, really smart. She gets good grades. She's also really good at art.

ADAM and I met when we were in third grade. Now that we're teenagers, we don't spend as much time together as we did when we were kids, but he's always there for me when I need him. (Plus, he's the only person who wants to talk about baseball with me!)

Characters

TOMMY's our class clown. Sometimes he's really funny, but sometimes he is just annoying. Becca has a crush on him . . . but I'd never tell.

I think **PETER** is probably the smartest person I've ever met. Seriously. He's even smarter than our teachers! He's also one of my friends. Which is lucky, because sometimes he helps me with homework.

Every school has a bully, and **JENNY** is ours. She's the tallest person in our class, and the meanest, too. She always threatens to stomp people. No one's ever seen her stomp anyone, but that doesn't mean it hasn't happened!

ANNA is the most popular girl at our school. Everyone wants to be friends with her. I think that's weird, because Anna can be really, really mean. I mostly try to stay away from her.

Cast of

CARLY is Anna's best friend. She always tries to act exactly like Anna does. She even wears the exact same clothes. She's never really been mean to me, but she's never been nice to me either!

CARLY

NICK is my annoying seven-year-old neighbor. I get stuck babysitting him a lot. He likes to make me miserable. (Okay, he's not that bad ALL of the time . . . just most of the time.)

NICK

SUSAN

SUSAN has never been a counselor at camp before, but I liked her the second I met her! She's tall, has red hair, and is really athletic. She's a freshman in college. She's the canoe instructor at camp too.

Characters

ROBERTA is the meanest girl at camp. She's even meaner than Jenny!

ROBERTA

DONNA

When I was a little kid, **DONNA** was my counselor. She's nice. She's the reason I want to be a junior counselor! She takes care of the little kids at camp.

MARY is the riding instructor at camp. She knows everything there is to know about horses.

MARY

RACHEL

I've been coming to camp for six years, and for four of them, **RACHEL** has been the swimming instructor. When I was a little kid, she taught me how to float!

CHAPTER 1

SUNDAY
Bus Ride

Every year, I look forward to the bus ride to camp. I like long bus rides with my friends. **We bring snacks, and we gossip and listen to each other's iPods.** But this year, I was on babysitting duty. Mom promised Mrs. Wright I'd keep an eye on her seven-year-old son. Nick lives next door, and he's never stayed overnight at a strange new place before.

"Ouch!" a girl squealed. "Nick pulled my hair!"

"I did not!" Nick stuck his tongue out.

"No pulling hair!" the bus driver yelled.

I don't think Blue River Camp is ready for Nick. **He likes being bad.** I've learned the hard way how to handle him. My mom babysits Nick a lot, but I end up watching him most of the time. Mom usually pays me two dollars an hour to watch Nick, but she wasn't paying me at all for the bus ride to camp. She said it was **just a nice thing to do.** I didn't have a choice.

"This year is going to be the best," Monica said. "I'm going to ride a real horse!"

I smiled at my **first best friend**. Monica is 𝐻𝒪𝑅𝒮𝐸 𝒞𝑅𝒜𝒵𝒴. She has a million little horse statues and tons of books about horses, but she's never ridden a horse. She's only ridden little ponies at the County Fair. Blue River Camp has a new barn and horses this year.

Becca sighed. "I don't care about horses. I hate camp," she said. **"A whole week without TV or the Internet? Ugh."**

Becca is my **second best friend**. She's not as daring as Monica and me, but she's smart. Becca never gets into trouble.

"I can't wait," Becca said. "After this week, **I won't ever have to go to camp again**."

We just finished seventh grade, so this is our last year at Blue River Camp. After this year we'll be too old. Eighth graders can only come back as junior counselors.

"I'll miss it," Monica said, "but if I like **horseback riding**, my parents will let me take lessons next summer."

I laughed. Monica wants to be a great Olympic rider someday. She never talks about anything else. "You will love horseback riding," I told her.

I LOVE CAMP. I have my heart set on being **Claudia Cortez, Junior Counselor.** Every summer the camp staff picks ten girls and ten boys to become junior counselors the next year. I think I have a good chance. I've been going to camp for six years, after all.

Also, I get along great with little kids. I'm used to Nick, and compared to him, **most little kids are angels.**

"Hey!" a boy in back yelled. "That's mine!"

"Catch!" Nick yelled back. He threw the kid's baseball cap. The boy got up to get it, and Nick stole the guy's seat.

"Move!" the boy complained. "That's my seat."

"**It's mine now**," Nick said.

"Quiet!" the bus driver yelled.

The boy let Nick have his seat. He probably didn't want to be in trouble with the driver. Nick didn't care.

Anyway, there are a lot of reasons I would make a good junior counselor. For example, some girls hate being outside. Not me. The nature hike is one of my favorite activities. I don't freak out about bugs and other creepy creatures. Icky things like **fungus and pond slime** don't give me the **HEEBIE-JEEBIES**.

Junior counselors also have to be trained swimmers. I'm a little worried about that. Last year, I didn't pass the long swim test to move up to the highest swim level. But the Harmon County Community Center in my hometown has an indoor pool, and I've been training.

I took a piece of gum out of my pocket. I started to pop it into my mouth. Then Jenny Pinski leaned over the back of my seat.

"I'll take that," Jenny said, holding out her hand.

Jenny is taller and stronger than all the girls at Pine Tree Middle School — and most of the boys, too. **She's meaner than everybody.**

I gave Jenny the gum, but **not because I was scared**. Okay, I was a little scared. I had another reason, though. I wouldn't be picked to be a junior counselor if I got into a fight.

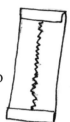

Monica nudged me. "**There go Anna and Carly**," she said, pointing out the window. A red car was passing the bus. Anna's brother Ben was driving. He plays basketball for the Pine Tree Eagles.

Becca stretched to see. "Maybe Anna and Carly aren't going to camp this year," she said.

"We're not that lucky," Monica said.

Anna is **bossy** and SELFISH. If she doesn't get her way, she makes everyone pay. She's also the most popular girl at our school. That doesn't make sense, but it's a fact of middle-school life. The cool kids get what they want.

I was sure that things would be different at camp.

"He pushed me!" the boy in the baseball cap shouted.

"You pushed me first!" Nick glared at the boy.

"That's it!" the bus driver yelled. She pulled off the road and stopped. Then she marched to the back of the bus.

The driver shook her finger in Nick's face and said, "The next time you cause trouble I'll take you off this bus. **No more pulling hair or shoving.** Do you understand?"

Nick nodded. He looked terrified. The driver wouldn't leave a little kid in the middle of the woods, but Nick didn't know that. I stored the driver's trick in my mind. I would have to use a line like that sometime when I was babysitting.

I wouldn't have to worry about Nick for seven whole days. Nick would be someone else's problem at Blue River Camp. **I couldn't wait until we got there.**

Claudia's Camp Survival Tip #1:

Bring extra gum for bullies and brats. And some for your friends!

Cougar Cabin

When the bus pulled into the camp parking lot, a tall older girl with red hair walked up. "I'm looking for **Claudia Cortez, Becca Robinson, and Monica Williams.** Any of them on this bus?" she asked the driver.

"I'm Claudia," I said, walking to the front of the bus. Monica and Becca followed me.

The older girl smiled. "Hi, Claudia!" she said. "I'm your counselor, Susan. You're in Cougar Cabin this summer."

"Cool!" I said. We grabbed our bags and started walking toward the cabin.

Susan walked next to me. "So, you're applying to be a junior counselor, right?" she asked. "I hope everything goes well for you this week!"

"Me too," I said happily. Things were off to a great start.

As soon as I walked into Cougar Cabin, **my stomach felt like it had rocks in it.**

Monica was right. Anna and Carly were already there. And they were staying in the same cabin with Becca, Monica, me, and three other girls.

Anna started bossing us around the second we walked into the cabin.

"Everyone better put their stuff away," she said. "I can't stand messes."

"Yeah!" Carly said. She goes along with everything Anna says.

I tried to ignore them. I looked around the room. There were four sets of bunk beds and one single bed, which was for Susan. "Which bunks should we take?" I asked Monica and Becca.

"Carly and I already claimed the bunks in the back corner," Anna said. **"It's too breezy by the windows."** She smiled sweetly. Then she tried to push her suitcase under the bunk, but it was too fat.

Everyone else had brought a smaller suitcase. Two suitcases were supposed to fit under each lower bunk. "Why don't you put yours against the wall, Anna?" Susan said. "It won't take up much room there."

"Thanks, Susan," Anna said. She grinned. "I couldn't get along for a whole week without my favorite things."

We had just gotten to camp, and **Anna was already getting special treatment,** just like at school. Nothing was different.

Monica, Becca, and I took the bunks in one front corner.

Each bunk had its own peg and shelf. I hung up my backpack, but I accidentally hung it upside down. It was unzipped, and everything fell out.

I jumped back and accidentally stepped on my toothpaste. The cap popped off and white toothpaste squirted out of the tube.

"Sorry," I said. My cheeks were red with embarrassment.

Everyone stared at me. Anna giggled. "Way to go, CLUMSY CLAUDIA. We've only been here for five minutes, and you're already making messes."

Monica and Becca helped me clean up. "Just ignore her, Claudia," Becca whispered.

I zipped my backpack and hung it up again, the right way this time.

Then I put my flashlight on the shelf and the shelf broke. All my stuff crashed to the floor.

"Really, Claudia. Try not to ruin the whole cabin," Anna said.

I turned red, but I wasn't too upset. **Good luck always evens out my bad luck.** Things would get better soon.

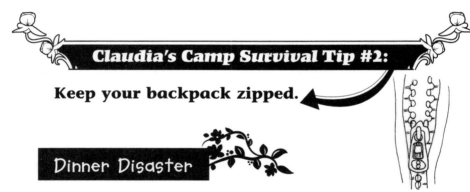

Claudia's Camp Survival Tip #2:

Keep your backpack zipped.

Dinner Disaster

The trail between our cabin and the mess hall, where we ate our meals, was very narrow. Trees lined both sides, and roots grew across the path. As we were walking to dinner, I tripped over a big root and **fell flat on my face.**

Becca almost tripped over me. She stopped  quickly, and Anna bumped into her.

"You made me stub my toe, Becca," Anna complained.

"Are you okay, Claudia?" Susan asked.

I nodded, but I was not okay. **I was mortified!** That's a word my grandma uses when she's really embarrassed. **I wanted to crawl into a hole and hide.**

I just laughed it off. "I'm fine." I stood up, 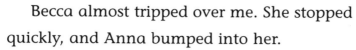 but some of the dirt on my knees and clothes wouldn't brush off.

"You're a mess, Claudia," Anna said.

"Well, we are going to the mess hall," I joked.

Everyone but Anna thought it was funny.

Becca and Monica were ahead of me in the food line. Anna, Carly, and the other Cougar girls were behind us.

"Don't stand too close to Claudia," Anna said. **"She might dump something on you."**

I acted like I didn't hear her, but I was extra careful while I picked up my food. I made it to our table without dropping my tray, and I didn't spill anything during the meal.

But my good luck wouldn't last. My fork slipped while I was cutting, and **a chunk of meat flew through the air.**

"Duck!" Carly yelled.

The chunk of meat sailed over Anna and the other girls. It landed in Adam's mashed potatoes at the next table.

Adam turned around and smiled. "Thanks, Claudia. I needed one more bite."

"You're welcome." I smiled back. Adam teases me sometimes, but he's never mean.

"Did you have to send it airmail?" Tommy joked.

Someone bumped into my chair just as I picked up my drink. I dropped the cup and **drowned my chocolate cake** in red fruit punch.

"Are you sure you're all right?" Monica asked, looking worried.

"She's a **walking danger zone,**" Anna said.

I ignored Anna and looked at Monica. "I'm just having one of those days."

"You can have half of my cake," Becca said.

When bad stuff happens I try to look on the bright side. The bright side about camp so far was that Monica and Becca were in Cougar Cabin with me, and that Jenny Pinski wasn't.

"Give me your cake," a girl said.

I looked at the table behind me. Jenny was sitting there. So was Roberta Diggs. I remembered Roberta from camp the year before.

Roberta is even bigger and meaner than Jenny. At our school, Jenny is famous for stomping people. I've never seen Jenny stomp anyone, but that doesn't mean it hasn't happened. At camp, **Roberta is famous for punching**. And I've seen it happen.

"Give it to me," Roberta said again.

Jenny gave Roberta her cake. She didn't want to get punched.

Claudia's Camp Survival Tip #3:

Eating can be dangerous. Don't make any sudden moves!

CHAPTER 2

MONDAY
Morning Mess

The next morning, I woke up suddenly. Then
I PANICKED. I had left my toothbrush in the
outhouse last night!

Each cabin group has a separate bathroom
building called an outhouse. It has showers, toilets,
and sinks. I knew I had left my toothbrush on one of
the sinks. If I went now, my toothbrush might still be
there. If I waited, the camp clean-up people might
throw it away.

Everyone already thought I was a hopeless klutz.
I did not want to be a hopeless klutz with bad breath!

I tiptoed to the door with my flashlight. The
door squeaked when I opened it, but no one in my
cabin woke up.

The sky was turning gray. I guessed that it was
about five a.m. The woods were still dark, and
my flashlight wasn't very bright. I didn't
want to fall again, so I walked slowly.

A twig SNAPPED.

I gasped.

An owl hooted.

My heart jumped.

Something shook the bushes.

I walked faster.

The outhouse didn't have lights. **It looked like a black hole in the woods.** But I was glad when I reached it.

The steps creaked.

That gave me chills.

I walked right into a spiderweb.

That made me shiver.

I clamped my mouth shut so I wouldn't scream. Then I wiped the sticky web off my face. My skin was cold and damp.

Usually, I'm not afraid of anything. But for some reason, **I was seriously creeped out**. It was really dark inside the outhouse. I paused in the doorway. If anything GROWLED, **roared, or screeched**, I was ready to run.

The only sound was water dripping in a sink. My toothbrush was on the counter where I had left it. I grabbed it and headed back to the cabin. **My luck had finally changed.**

The sun was starting to rise, and I could see the trail a little better. The morning wake-up song hadn't played yet over the loudspeakers to wake up all the campers. I could get back in bed and no one would ever know I left.

Except Susan, who was outside looking for me. GREAT.

"Claudia!" Susan called. Her hair was a mess. Her sneakers were untied, and she was wearing pajamas. **She looked really worried.**

When she saw me, at first, Susan was relieved. "Thank goodness you're all right," she said.

Then she was worried again. "Where were you?" she asked, putting her hands on her hips.

"The outhouse," I said. "I realized I left my toothbrush there."

"Claudia, **you really scared me.** Campers are not allowed to leave the cabin in the dark! I thought you were lost in the woods," Susan said.

"I had my flashlight." I held up my flashlight. "And I found my toothbrush." I held up my toothbrush.

Susan wasn't impressed. "Claudia, you know the rules. **Don't do that again.**"

"I won't," I said. "Promise."

I had my toothbrush, so I didn't have to worry about bad breath. But now I had to worry that my counselor thought I was a KLUTZ and a TROUBLEMAKER.

The camp has never given a **Worst Camper Of The Week** award. But if they did, I'd probably win it. At the rate I was going, I was never going to be chosen to be a junior counselor.

Claudia's Camp Survival Tip #4:

Bring an extra toothbrush and toothpaste.

Sink or Swim

Every year, the counselors and instructors study the seventh graders who want to be junior counselors. They knew who we were because each of us filled out a form before we came to camp. The counselors were supposed to take notes and grade our skills and attitudes. **We didn't know what was important or when we were being judged.**

The only thing we knew for sure is that we had to pass all the swimming tests. The first round of tests was Monday morning.

Junior counselors help the campers practice what the instructors teach, and they stand watch like lifeguards during free swims. They have to be advanced swimmers. The swimming test was the most important thing I had to do to become a junior counselor. **If I didn't do well, I wouldn't make it.**

I had butterflies in my stomach when I got to the lake. Becca and Monica came with me to cheer me on.

"Don't worry," Monica said. "You've trained all year for this."

"Yep." I shook my arms to loosen up.

"You'll be great," Becca added. "I just know it."

"Yep," I said. I wasn't sure I believed her. **The more I want something, the more nervous I get.**

I **REALLY** wanted to be a junior counselor.

"Wish me luck," I said. **I smiled at my friends and took a deep breath.** Then I walked over to where Anna and fourteen other junior counselor candidates were standing on the dock.

The swimming area is divided into three parts. The dock is shaped like the letter H. The shallow water by the beach is for the beginners. They're called Puppies, because beginner swimmers usually dog paddle. A rope separates the **PUPPY** section from the intermediate section. Intermediate swimmers are Mutts. Advanced swimmers were called K-9s.

The dock in the middle of the H dock separates the intermediate and advanced sections. The water in that section is too deep to stand.

The swimming instructor's name was Rachel. She walked in front of us. She was wearing an orange swimming suit and was carrying a clipboard.

"Okay, guys, it looks like ten of you are already K-9s," Rachel said. "You're excused this period."

The K-9 swimmers cheered and ran off. I stayed where I was. I didn't finish the long swim last year. **I was still a Mutt**. Anna was a Mutt too.

"The first test is treading water for five minutes," Rachel said. "In the K-9 area, where you can't touch the bottom."

We all jumped in. **I squealed.** Lake water is cold!

Rachel let us warm up. Then she started her stopwatch. "Go!" she shouted.

Treading water is EASY. You just move your arms and legs around so you don't SINK.

Anna splashed to stay afloat, and she almost sank three times. **She even swallowed water and had to cough it up.**

I wasn't even breathing very hard when Rachel blew her whistle.

"Is five minutes up already?" Anna asked as we climbed out of the water. "It only seemed like one." She fixed her ponytail.

"That means you didn't use much energy, Anna," Rachel said. "Good job."

I thought she was kidding. No one said anything nice to me. **My stomach twisted into a knot.**

Next we had to swim across the Mutt section three times. Each time across is called a lap. We had to use a different stroke on each lap.

Rachel made us line up in lanes. **I got stuck between Anna and the rope that marks off the Puppy section.**

We were supposed to swim overhand first and breaststroke second. I did those just fine. But on the third lap, we switched to the backstroke.

It's hard to tell where you're going when you're swimming backward.

I glanced from side to side to keep myself moving in a straight line. **I was shocked when my arm hit Anna.** She had veered into my lane.

"Watch it!" Anna squealed.

"Sorry!" I exclaimed. **I almost messed up and touched the bottom.**

At the end of the race, Anna finished first. "I can't believe I beat everyone," she said, fixing her ponytail. "Especially after Claudia barged into my lane."

"Be careful, Claudia," Rachel said. "It's not fair to crowd the others."

I watched Susan pat Anna on the back. The other girls gave her high fives. I didn't want to make everyone think I was a poor sport or a sore loser. So I let it go.

The knot in my stomach got tighter.

The long swim was next. It was ten laps. Last year I only finished seven laps.

This time I tried to remember everything I'd learned at the pool in my hometown's community center. I took long strokes instead of short ones to go farther with less work. I didn't lift my head to breathe. **That's tiring and slows you down.** Instead, I turned my head to the side just enough to take in air.

We could use any stroke for the long swim. We could even float or tread water to catch our breath. But we couldn't touch the bottom until we finished ten laps.

I started to get pretty tired after five laps. I turned on my back and did the frog kick my dad taught me. I was resting and moving at the same time.

Then a leg cramp took me by surprise. **It felt like a giant lobster claw had clamped onto my left leg.** It hurt so much. I grabbed my leg and cried out.

Rachel dove in and pulled me back to the dock. "Oh, Claudia, you poor thing," she said when we were on dry ground.

I managed to make a weak smile.
"I'm okay," I said.

My pride hurt more than my leg did. I had
failed the long swim test. At least I could try again
tomorrow.

Claudia's Camp Survival Tip #5:

**Don't go to camp with Anna. Oh, and a
good way to get rid of a leg cramp is to walk
really carefully until the pain starts to go
away.**

Horsing Around

"Don't you want to watch me ride a horse
for the very first time?" Monica asked Becca
later that day. We were in our cabin during free time.

"I want to, but I can't," Becca said. "I'm going on a
hike. We have to write down all the different birds we
see in a journal."

"You should be good at that," I said. Becca keeps a journal at home. She writes in it every single night.

"I picked the hike because **I don't feel like getting dirty** or catching bugs," Becca explained. "Peter signed up, too."

Peter is the smartest kid in the seventh grade at Pine Tree Middle School. He's also one of our friends.

"Then you *HAVE TO* come with me, Claudia," Monica said. She held out a camera. "Someone has to take my picture."

I hesitated. I needed to practice swimming, but **I couldn't let down my friend.**

"Okay. I wouldn't miss your first time riding, Monica," I said.

We walked over to the riding area together. The riding instructor stood by the door of the big red barn with a big brown horse. Six other horses were saddled and tied in the corral. There were three boys and three girls in the class with Monica.

"Well, **my dream is about to come true,**" Monica said. She beamed with excitement. "Maybe you should take a lot of pictures. To make sure we get a good one."

"Okay," I said. I sat on a big log to wait. The instructor was showing the class how to brush the horses.

Something PINCHED my leg. I felt a second **pinch** and a third and then a bunch more. I jumped up. **The log was covered with ants!** They were all over my legs.

I brushed off the tiny critters, and the pinching stopped. **Then the bites started to itch.**

I couldn't go see the camp nurse, because I had to take Monica's picture. So I waited and scratched.

After a couple of minutes, the youngest group of boys and girls walked past me. The first and second graders are called the Wolf Pack. Nick was in the Wolf Pack.

"Are we going to ride a horse, Donna?" a girl asked.

"Nope. We're going ride in a wagon," the counselor said.

"That's no fun," another girl said.

The counselor grinned. "It's a covered wagon pulled by a big, fat pony named Baby."

All the kids perked up. That's one thing I really like about little kids. **They're really easy to please.**

Then I noticed Nick. He was walking way behind the other kids. His shoulders were slumped. He dragged his feet. **He looked totally lost and alone.**

"What's the matter, Nick?" I asked.

"Claudia?" Nick's head snapped up. He sort of smiled.

I almost fainted. Was Nick happy to see me? Then I got worried. **Nick and I can't stand each other.** "Are you sick?" I asked him.

Nick sniffled back a tear. "I miss my mom."

Nick wasn't sick. **He was homesick!** No wonder he was happy to see me.

"I want to go home," Nick whined.

"Don't you want to ride in the covered wagon first?" I asked him.

Nick sniffled again and nodded. Then he followed me to the shed. Monica's class was still learning how to put a saddle and bridle on their horses, so I had plenty of time.

Donna was surprised to see me. She was more surprised when **I told Nick to sit down and he did it.** He pushed two other kids off the bale of hay, but he sat.

"I've been looking for a VOLUNTEER," Donna said. "To watch the kids while I'm getting Baby and the wagon ready. Do you want the job?"

"Yes!" I said. **I couldn't believe my luck.** Watching younger campers was PERFECT for someone who wanted to be a junior counselor. **I love little kids.** Plus, I could hang out at the barn with Monica.

It took ten minutes to hitch the pony, Baby, to the wagon. By then, Nick had gotten over being homesick. **He stuffed straw down a boy's shirt and pulled the petals off a girl's wildflower.**

I made Nick sit by himself and helped the boy shake the straw out of his shirt. Then I took the girl's picture so she'd stop crying.

"Thank you so much," Donna said. "I couldn't have done this without you. Do you want to come along for the wagon ride?"

"I wish I could," I said. Monica had waited her whole life to ride a horse. I had to capture the moment with a picture. She would treasure it forever.

I went back to the barn. All the kids were on horses in the corral. Monica was sitting on a big, brown horse. She wasn't moving.

I raised the camera, but I didn't push the button.

Monica looked terrified. "I can't do this, Mary," Monica told the instructor. "I feel like I'm going to fall off and get squashed."

"Just remember, the horse is trained to pay attention to people," Mary said. "Horses are big, but people are smarter."

"People can't squash a horse," Monica said.

"And **horses don't squash people**," Mary said with a smile. She grabbed the rope that was clipped to the bridle of Monica's horse.

Mary tugged the rope, and the horse took a step. "Come on, Rocky," Mary said softly.

Monica bit her lip and hung on to the saddle as Mary led Rocky around the corral. I knew this wasn't how she imagined her first horse ride. But first times only happen once.

I took the picture.

Claudia's Camp Survival Tip #6:

If you're wearing shorts, watch where you sit!

CHAPTER 3

TUESDAY
Stressful Swamp

On Tuesday morning, I woke up feeling REALLY EXCITED. It was Nature Hike Day! The nature hike was one of my favorite things to do at camp. I like it so much I wasn't even upset that Anna, Jenny, and Roberta were going, too.

"You can still change your mind about the nature hike, Becca," I said as I sprayed bug spray on my legs.

"No, thanks." Becca held up a plastic pail. "I'd rather pick blueberries with Carly then touch bugs and stuff. And the cook promised to make blueberry pies from the berries we pick. See you later!" She rushed out of the cabin. **The screen door slammed behind her.**

The nature hike led us to a clearing in the woods. We looked for interesting plants and rocks. We took pictures of the insects we caught. Then we let them go.

"This is a beautiful butterfly!" Anna put the lid on her jar. The lid had air holes. "It will look GREAT with these wildflowers."

Anna wanted to be a junior counselor as much as I did. Only ten girls would be chosen, and we had to be outstanding to make it.

I don't like Anna, but I gave her some advice.

"Butterflies and wildflowers are **pretty**, but they aren't **unusual** or **exciting**," I said. "Everybody's collecting them."

Anna looked around. Most of the other girls had caught butterflies and picked flowers too. Even Jenny and Roberta.

"What do you have?" Anna asked.

"A cricket, a pinecone, and a tree fungus." I showed her the fungus. It was shaped like a half circle. One side was smooth and white. "Look, you can write on it with a stick. The marks turn brown," I said. I showed her.

Anna frowned. "**I have to find one of those.**"

We kept hiking. Soon, we stopped in a wet, open area. "This is a swamp," Susan said. The ground was **solid** in some parts and **squishy** in other parts. I found a few frogs in a small pool. I waded in the shallow water to catch one.

"Help!" Anna squealed behind me. She was leaning over and trying to catch a frog without getting her feet wet. **She almost fell face down in the water.**

"The water isn't deep, Anna," I said.

"I'm wearing brand-new sneakers," Anna explained. "My mom will be mad if I ruin them."

I was trying to be helpful to prove I'd be a good junior counselor. So I caught the frog for Anna. **She didn't even thank me.** She just left.

I turned to catch a frog for myself. But there weren't any more. I guess they had all taken off.

Then I heard a shriek. I looked over and saw that Monica was standing on one leg. "What are you doing, Monica?" I asked.

Monica pushed her hair out of her face. "My shoe's stuck in the mud," she said. She looked upset. She kept trying to bend over and pick up the shoe without falling into the mud.

I walked over to her. Then I took off my shoes and socks and stuck my foot in the mud. **The mud and slimy water felt good on my itchy ant bites.** I used my toes to find Monica's shoe.

"Thanks, Claudia," Monica said. She slipped her shoe back on. She looked relieved. Susan saw what had happened. She smiled at me.

Jenny was standing in a puddle full of tadpoles. She was trying to scoop them into a jar. Her face was spattered with mud, and her clothes were soaked. Roberta was sitting on a rock behind her, **shouting orders.** "Move to the left! No, more to the left! Scoop more up, Jenny!" she was yelling. Roberta's clothes were perfectly clean.

Anna finally found a tree fungus and showed it to Susan. "Look! You can write on it with a stick," Anna said. She used a twig to print her name on the white side. The letters turned brown.

"Wow!" Susan exclaimed. **"That is so cool!"**

I just sighed.

We were almost back to our cabins when my luck changed. A small grass snake slithered across the trail in front of me.

I didn't stop to think. I POUNCED and grabbed it.

"That's so cool!" Monica said, coming over to look.

"Claudia can't be a junior counselor if she's not a K-9 swimmer," Anna said under her breath. "So it doesn't matter how good she is at finding nature stuff."

Anna gets nasty when she's annoyed. But she had a point.

As we walked up to the cabins, the blueberry pickers were just getting back.

"I hope you guys found enough blueberries for a lot of pies," Roberta said. "**I could eat a whole one all by myself.**"

The blueberry pickers turned over their pails. They were all **empty.**

"We looked and looked," Carly said, "but we couldn't find any blueberries."

I was SUSPICIOUS. I had seen blueberries the day before!

Then I noticed something.

Everyone in the blueberry group had blue stains around their mouths. **They had eaten all the blueberries.**

Claudia's Camp Survival Tip #7:

Blueberry juice leaves stains.

Water Hound

I still had to pass the long swim test. **Anna was right.** It didn't matter if I was a nature-hike star. I had to be a good swimmer if I wanted to be a junior counselor.

So after we got back from the hike, I changed into my swimsuit and started walking to the lake.

"You can do it, you can do it," I said over and over as I walked to the lake.

Jenny was on the dock. She was waiting for Rachel too.

"Are you trying to be a junior counselor?" I asked. **I was pretty sure the camp staff wouldn't pick a bully.**

"No," Jenny answered. "I just want to be a K-9."

"Why?" I asked. It wasn't like Jenny to have goals.

"Because Roberta is a terrible swimmer," Jenny explained. "She'll never get into the deep water."

Suddenly I understood. Roberta picked on Jenny, so Jenny wanted to get away from Roberta. **Jenny was used to being a bully, but she wasn't used to being bullied!**

Then Anna walked over to me.

"Aren't you tired after the nature hike, Claudia?" Anna asked. "What if you fail the long swim again? You can only take it three times."

I knew that. **Anna was just trying to shake my confidence.** I didn't answer her question.

"What are those red bumps on your legs?"
Anna asked.

"Ant bites," I said. The bites started itching.

I scratched. That made the ant bites itchier.

Rachel walked up with her clipboard. "You've passed two of the tests, Claudia," she said. "There are two more to go. Do you want to try the underwater swim first?"

I nodded. The underwater test was only one lap. That would help me warm up for the long swim.

My dad had taught me how to hold my breath longer. Most people take one or two deep breaths when they're getting ready to go underwater. **My dad taught me to take lots of short breaths.** That stores more oxygen, and you don't let all your air out too fast.

I swam a whole lap without coming up to breathe.

"Great job, Claudia!" Rachel said as I pulled myself up onto the dock. "Why don't you take a quick break. Jenny, it's your turn for the underwater test."

I sat on the dock and scratched my bug bites while Jenny swam.

Anna walked over and stood near me. "Don't worry, Claudia," Anna said. "The long swim is only ten laps. You **probably** won't get a leg cramp today."

Anna wanted everyone to think she was trying to make me feel better. She wasn't. **She was trying to make me nervous.** Well, it wouldn't work.

After everyone was done with the underwater test, Jenny, two other girls, and I started the long swim.

After four laps, I was still swimming strong. I wasn't tired at all. Then Jenny lurched sideways and slammed into me. **I was surprised, so I accidentally put my foot down.**

It happened so fast that nobody noticed. But I knew I'd done it, and I knew it was **against the rules.**

I stopped, swam back to the dock, and told Rachel that I touched the bottom. I didn't blame Jenny. It wouldn't change anything, and Jenny might decide to get even.

"Thank you for being 𝐻𝒪𝒩𝐸𝒮𝒯, Claudia," Rachel said. "You're out this time, but you can try again on Friday, okay?"

"You only swam four laps this time," Anna said as she walked away. "Maybe you should just give up now."

Sometimes I don't succeed, but I never give up.

"I can do it, Rachel," I said. "I know I can."

Rachel smiled. "I know you can too, Claudia. You can try again on Friday."

"I'll be here." I scratched the itchy ant bites.

"Go see the nurse," Rachel said.

Claudia's Camp Survival Tip #8:

A paste made from baking soda mixed with water makes bug bites stop itching.

CHAPTER 4

WEDNESDAY
Craft Corner

After breakfast on Wednesday, it started to RAIN. At first it was just a drizzle. Then it started to **pour**. So the counselors told us we'd have Arts and Crafts.

"I can't believe Jenny signed up to make a birdhouse!" Becca said, staring at the sign-up sheets. We could choose from making jewelry, building a birdhouse, or working on the pottery wheel.

I was disappointed. When I'm at camp, I like being outside. I hoped the rain went away by the next day, because I was signed up for canoeing.

"Jenny was almost nice to me yesterday," I said.

"That's hard to believe," Becca said.

Just then, Jenny came over. "Can I work with you guys? I don't know any of these other dorks."

Becca looked at me. I shrugged, so she mumbled, "Okay."

"Do you like birds, Jenny?" I asked.

"Not really," Jenny said. "But Roberta's back in our cabin. **She hates crafts.** That's why I'm here."

Jenny went over to the table in the middle of the cabin. The table was covered with lots of different kinds of supplies. Becca whispered, **"I almost feel sorry for her."**

"Yeah," I agreed. "Now Jenny knows what it feels like to be bullied."

"Then maybe she'll stop." Becca grinned.

Jenny came back and shoved some yarn into my hands. "Here, I got this for you," she said. Jenny was actually being nice. **It was weird.**

Horse Play

After an hour in the Arts and Crafts cabin, it finally stopped raining. I decided to see if Nick's counselor, Donna, needed any help with the little kids, Baby, and the wagon. I stopped at the barn to see Monica first.

The other kids were riding horses in the corral, but Monica was in the barn ALONE, cleaning a saddle.

"Why aren't you riding?" I asked.

"Well, uh . . ." Monica looked away. "Rocky isn't feeling well."

"Can't you ride another horse?" I asked.

"Rocky's my favorite," Monica said.

Monica has been my best friend since first grade. I know when she's keeping something from me.

Monica was afraid to ride.

Claudia's Camp Survival Tip #9:

Rainy day at camp? Don't worry. Arts and Crafts is a great time to make presents for your parents. Parents love homemade stuff.

Marshmallow Monster

That night was campfire night, my **favorite** camp tradition.

Becca, Monica, and I were walking down the trail to the bonfire area. "**I'm so excited.** I love the campfire," I said. I aimed my flashlight at the trail. It was almost dark.

"I like toasting marshmallows and singing," Becca said, "but the ghost stories kind of **freak me out.**"

"They're just stories," Monica said.

"If you get too scared, Tommy will protect you," I teased. Only Monica and I know that **Becca likes Tommy.**

There were several benches around a huge bonfire in a clearing. The three of us sat with Adam, Tommy, and Peter. They had a big bag of marshmallows, plus graham crackers and chocolate for s'mores.

While we all roasted marshmallows, Adam told a creepy story about a grizzly bear ghost that wanted its claws back. Tommy flirted with Becca. Peter wondered if science could prove ghosts were real. I ate about seventeen s'mores.

Monica just stared at the fire. **She looked sad.**
I knew why. She couldn't be a great rider if she was
afraid of horses.

I wanted to help, but **I didn't know what to do.**

Across the clearing, I watched Donna, Nick's
counselor, walk over and sit down next to him. The
marshmallow on the end of Nick's stick was burning.
Donna grabbed the stick out of Nick's hand.

"Don't do that!" Nick shrieked.

Donna blew out Nick's flaming marshmallow.
She put it in a paper napkin and handed it to him.
"They taste better if they're not burnt," Donna said.

"I don't want to eat it!" Nick threw the
marshmallow in the fire. **"I want it to burn."**

He put another marshmallow on his stick. Then
Nick stuck the new marshmallow in the fire. It burst
into flames. **Then the gooey glob fell off the stick
into the fire.**

"I lost my marshmallow!" Nick screeched.

That was my cue. I took the s'more supplies and
walked over to Nick.

"You can let it burn and lose it," I told him as I handed over a new marshmallow. "Or you can blow out the flames and eat it. Or, you might like s'mores," I said.

"What's a s'more?" Nick asked.

I whispered in his ear, "It's an old camping recipe. With chocolate and cookies. **It's a secret, so you can't tell anyone.**"

"I won't," Nick whispered back.

"Good. Blow out your marshmallow." I smiled at Nick's counselor. Donna nodded and gave me a thumbs-up.

I kept Nick happy and quiet. We burned marshmallows to a crisp and ate chocolate graham cracker sandwiches.

Claudia's Camp Survival Tip #10:

Campfire light attracts bugs. Don't forget the bug spray.

As we walked back to the cabin after the campfire, I told Becca and Monica I had to talk to them. "It's an EMERGENCY," I said. "But I can't tell you what it's about until later. I'll sneak out after everyone's asleep. Wait ten minutes, and then meet me at the barn."

Monica frowned. "Why are we meeting at the barn?" she asked.

"Horses can't tell anyone what we say," I explained.

Everyone was tired and **stuffed with marshmallows.** Even Susan fell asleep right away.

After everyone fell asleep, I quietly slipped outside and went to the barn. No one was there but the horses.

I had learned a lot about horses when I was helping Donna with Baby. All the camp horses are safe for kids. They don't kick, bite, buck, or get scared easily. **I had to show Monica that Rocky wouldn't hurt her.**

I was ready when Monica and Becca arrived.

"Claudia?" Monica called. "Where are you?"

"Over here!" I whispered loudly. "In Rocky's stall."

The stall was narrow. I stood all the way in by Rocky's head. The BIG horse didn't mind. He just munched his hay.

"What are you doing in there?" Monica asked.

"I thought I heard a cat," I lied. **I hate to lie, but I had a plan.** "I came in to rescue it," I added.

"Where's the cat?" Becca asked.

"There wasn't one," I said. "But now I need to be rescued. I'm afraid to walk past Rocky. **He might squash me.**"

"My instructor told me that **horses don't squash people,**" Monica said.

"Ever?" Becca asked. "Or just mostly."

"I don't know." Monica shrugged.

"I can't stay here," I said. "If I get caught, **they won't let me be a junior counselor.**"

I had broken the rules. We're not supposed to be outside at night. But **Monica's lifelong dream was more important than being a junior counselor.**

"You have to help me, Monica," I pleaded.

Monica made a clucking sound and touched Rocky's rump. "It's just me, Rocky. Move over." She clucked and pushed until Rocky moved. "C'mon, Claudia."

I inched along the wall and pretended to be scared. When I was out, **I pretended to be really relieved.**

Rocky made a low rumbling sound. Monica went into the stall and rubbed him under the chin.

"I didn't realize Rocky was so easy to push around," Monica said.

"So you're not afraid anymore?" I asked.

Monica grinned. **"I guess not."**

"What's the other emergency, Claudia?" Becca asked. "The one you called the meeting for."

"This was it," I confessed. "I wanted to help Monica get over being afraid of horses. And it worked!"

Claudia's Camp Survival Tip #11:

One of the most important things about camp is being a good friend!

CHAPTER 5

THURSDAY
Saddles and Secrets

The next morning, I went back to the barn with Monica.

"I'm going to ride Rocky today," Monica told Mary.

Her instructor smiled. "That's **wonderful!**"

Monica had paid attention to everything she'd learned in class. She brushed Rocky and cleaned his hooves. Then she saddled and bridled him. She even led him out of the barn to the corral.

Monica had **one nervous moment** right before she got on Rocky's back. She looked at Mary and asked, "Are you sure he won't run away with me?"

Mary laughed. "Yes. **Rocky is too lazy to run away.**"

I stayed to take more pictures. This time Monica sat up straight and smiled. **She looked like a real rider.**

"This is just as *MUCH FUN* as I thought it would be!" Monica called to me. She nudged Rocky's side with her heel. He started to jog. Monica bounced, but she didn't fall off.

I found Becca in our cabin and told her the good news.

"I'm glad you tricked Monica last night," Becca said. "**She loves horses more than anything.** It would have been so sad if she didn't learn to ride."

"I knew she could do it," I said.

"And we know you can do the long swim," Becca said. "You just have to believe it, Claudia."

I knew she was right. **I just had to convince myself** that I really could do it.

Claudia's Camp Survival Tip #12:

When friends give you good advice, take it.

Tip A Canoe

I ran down the trail to the lake. I couldn't stop thinking about what Becca had said. I did believe in myself.

My luck was just worse than usual.

And it wasn't changing. The ant bites were still itchy, and Susan paired me up with **Anna.**

"Paddling a canoe can't be that hard," Anna said. We stood on the beach with eight other campers.

"There's a right way and a wrong way," Susan said. She sat in the back of a canoe and paddled on the right side. The canoe went in a circle to the left.

"How do you get it to go straight?" I asked.

"It's easy with **two people** in a canoe. Each of you has a paddle, so there's a paddle on both sides," Susan explained. "When you're **alone**, you have to use a **J-paddle.**"

The J-paddle had three parts. First, Susan dipped the paddle in the water. Then she pulled the wide side toward her.

Then she pushed the edge side out and the wide side forward. The pattern made a backward ℑ in the water.

"Switching the paddle from side to side keeps the canoe going straight, too," Susan said. "But that's very tiring."

Each of us put on a lifejacket and picked up a paddle.

"I'm sitting in front," Anna said as she got into our canoe. **"I want to make sure you don't run into anything, Claudia."**

That was okay with me. If Anna was watching the water, she wouldn't be bossing me around.

She complained instead. She said:

1. The seat was too hard.

2. The paddle was too heavy.

3. Her arms hurt.

4. The sun was too hot.

5. There were too many bugs.

I enjoyed the trip across the lake. It was quiet and peaceful when Anna wasn't talking. The canoe glided through the water, and paddling was fun.

Then we turned around to go back.

"I'm too tired to paddle anymore." Anna put her paddle across the front of the canoe. "Just do that **J-paddle** thing."

If I refused to paddle by myself, Anna would tell everyone I got us **stuck in the middle of the lake**.

> Weird Law of the Universe: If there are two versions of the same story, most people will believe the worst.

J-paddling wasn't hard, but it **slowed us down.** The others beat us back and pulled their canoes onto the beach.

We weren't far from shore, though. I could see that the little kids were fishing from the dock. The counselors didn't see Nick get into a canoe with his fishing pole. **The canoe wasn't tied up very well, and it began to drift away from shore.**

I didn't shout a warning. I didn't want to scare Nick. I steered toward the loose canoe with Nick in it.

"Hi, Claudia!" Nick waved when we got closer.

"Where's your paddle, kid?" Anna asked.

Nick looked around. "I don't have a paddle!"

"Just stay calm and sit still," I said.

Nick hardly ever does what I tell him. He PANICKED and stood up. The canoe tipped, and **he fell into the lake.**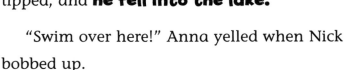

"Swim over here!" Anna yelled when Nick bobbed up.

Nick could dog paddle, but the beach was too far. **I ripped off my lifejacket and threw it to him.** He grabbed the jacket and hung on. Then he kicked to reach our canoe.

"C'mon, kid. You can do it." Anna held out her hand.

"No!" I yelled. I paddled our canoe away from Nick. The canoe would tip if he tried to get in. **Then we'd all have to swim for our lives.**

Anna gasped. "What are you doing?"

I ignored Anna and headed toward the beach. "Keep kicking, Nick. We're almost there."

"Help me, Claudia!" Nick swallowed water and sputtered.

"Don't talk!" I shouted. "Swim!" If Nick let go of the lifejacket, I would jump in to save him. But he held on.

When we reached the beach, Donna pulled Nick out of the water. "Are you all right?" she asked.

"No," Nick said. He was crying. "I almost DROWNED. Claudia wouldn't pull me out of the lake."

Then Susan said something that **shocked** me. "I want everyone to know that Claudia did exactly the right thing. If Claudia had let Nick climb into the canoe, it could have tipped over. Then she and Anna would have been in trouble, too," she explained. "**Claudia saved Nick** without putting herself or Anna in danger."

The campers clapped and cheered.

Claudia's Camp Survival Tip #13:

Don't put yourself in danger to save someone else from drowning.

Lies And Ivy

Nick's scary adventure was the **big news** at dinner.

"You're a *HERO*, Claudia," Monica said.

Anna disagreed. "She is not. **Claudia didn't dive in to save Nick.**"

"She gave him her lifejacket," Becca said.

"She wouldn't let him get in our canoe," Anna argued. But everyone ignored her.

After dinner, I took a cookie to Nick. The nurse made him stay in her office during dinner so she could keep an eye on him. He wouldn't admit he was scared or lonely. I thought **cookies might make him feel better.**

As I was walking up to the nurse's office door, Jenny was walking out. Her arms and legs were covered with spots of pink lotion.

"What happened?" I asked.

Jenny said, "I jumped off the trail and hid so Roberta couldn't find me. I got tangled up in poison ivy vines."

My luck had been mostly BAD all week. Just about everyone thought I was a klutz, and I had failed the swimming test twice. But at least I didn't have poison ivy!

Claudia's Camp Survival Tip #14:

Poison oak and poison ivy have three leaves. Don't touch them!

CHAPTER 6

FRIDAY
Breakfast Hunt

On Friday morning, some of us were SAD and some of us were GLAD. It was our last day at camp.

Becca was glad. She wanted to go home. She was going to start a bird-watching club at school. Peter had already promised to join.

Monica was sad to leave Rocky, but she was excited to take riding lessons next summer.

I was sad and nervous. I had been coming to Blue River Camp for seven years. I had to pass the long swim test or I couldn't come back next summer as a junior counselor. Today was my last chance.

We brushed our teeth and then headed to the mess hall for breakfast. When we got there, the cook was wearing his pajamas, and his hair was sticking up. "I am so sorry," he said. "The kitchen staff overslept."

"I'm starving!" someone yelled. "What are we going to eat?"

"We'll have to **search** for food," Donna said.

The campers were shocked. We had to find our own breakfast in the **wild!**

Donna asked me to help with the little kids. I think she just wanted me to keep Nick out of trouble.

"Some wild plants are bad to eat," Donna told the kids. "Like toadstools and mushrooms." She pointed to some spotted red toadstools. "It's too hard to tell the good ones from the bad ones."

"Bad!" Nick stomped on a toadstool.

I stopped him before he flattened the others. The toadstools belonged in the woods. They weren't hurting anyone.

"You're no fun, Claudia." Nick tried to kick me. I jumped out of reach.

When Nick touched a plant with red berries, Donna yelled, "Nick! Don't."

"My tummy's growling," Nick complained.

"You don't want to eat those berries," Donna said.

"Are they **deadly?**" I asked.

"No," Donna said, "but they'll make you very sick."

Soon we found some blueberry bushes. The little kids ate all the blueberries they could reach, but it didn't fill them up.

"I want a DOUGHNUT," Nick said. **"And orange juice."**

"Doughnuts and O.J. don't grow in the woods," I said.

"Can we catch a **fish?**" a little girl asked.

"We didn't catch one yesterday," a boy said.

"And we don't have a fire to cook it," another boy said.

A girl started to cry. "I'm hungry."

"I smell **doughnuts.**" Nick sniffed the air.

"Let's follow Nick's nose," Donna said. She smiled.

Nick led the way down a trail. Pretty soon I smelled doughnuts, too. And sausage! **I thought I was so hungry that I was imagining things.**

Then we stepped into a clearing.

Breakfast was served in the woods!

"SURPRISE!" The cooks, Becca, and a few other older campers yelled. They stood behind tables that were piled with doughnuts, orange juice, sausage, and eggs.

Everyone was starving after walking through the woods. I was hungry too, but I didn't eat much. I just had a small dish of eggs and a glass of orange juice. I didn't want to try the long swim on a full stomach. This was my last chance to pass the test.

Claudia's Camp Survival Tip #15:

Don't eat anything that grows wild. It's better to be safe than sick.

Swim Test

A big crowd came to the lake to watch me swim. Donna brought Nick and the little kids. All my friends were there, too.

"We're rooting for you, Claudia!" Adam shouted.

"Relax and take your time," Rachel told me.

"You can do it, Claudia," Susan said.

It helped to know my counselor and swimming instructor believed in me. I felt more confident as I dove into the water. Nothing could stop me from passing this time. Not Anna or a cramp or a pulled muscle.

"Go for it, Claudia!" Becca and Monica yelled.

I swam overhand and backstroke for the first five laps. Then I started to get tired. I could hear everyone urging me on. I floated for a few seconds to rest. Then I swam again.

I swam, treaded water, floated, and dog paddled, but I kept going. I lost track of the laps.

When Rachel reached in to pull me out, I thought it was a mistake.

"No, no! I'm okay!" I argued. "I can do it!"

"You did do it, Claudia!" Rachel exclaimed. "You just finished swimming ten laps."

"You're a K-9!" Susan yelled.

"I am?" I leaped into the air and WHOOPED.

Passing the long swim test was definitely a jumping-for-joy occasion.

Claudia's Camp Survival Tip #16:

Believe in yourself.

Awards Dinner

The Awards Dinner was the last big event of the week. **All the campers look forward to it.** The staff serves a YUMMY meal, and there are prizes. **Everyone** wants to win something. There were ribbons and trophies on a long table.

"Every year I hope I get something," Becca said. "But I never do."

"I don't either," Monica said.

I really **wanted to win a camp award too.**

"Last year I won a ribbon for having the neatest bunk," Anna said. "And the year before that I got a trophy for the best leaf collection."

Adam cut her off. "We should give the cook an award for these mashed potatoes. They're the *BEST* I've ever had."

We had hot fudge sundaes for dessert. Then the counselors and the instructors gave out the awards.

Peter won a trophy for **Best Sport.** He gets teased for being brainy and not very athletic, but he never gets upset.

Becca won a blue ribbon for the **Best Birdhouse.**

Monica won a set of silver spurs for being the **Most Improved Rider.**

"I can't believe it!" Monica gasped. "I'm going to hang them on my wall. I don't want to use them on a horse."

I got a trophy for being the Camper Who Wouldn't Give Up. **I was thrilled!**

Finally, it was time to give out the top honors. All the counselors and instructors voted for the winners.

Adam won a trophy for the Best All-Around Camper. He was amazed. Anna was **amazed** and FURIOUS because she didn't win anything.

No one was more amazed than me when Susan announced that I had been voted the **Most Valuable Camper.**

The trophy was HUGE!

Claudia's Camp Survival Tip #17:

Sometimes bad luck is good luck in disguise.

CHAPTER 7

P.S.

After the Awards Dinner, the counselors told me that taking care of Nick was one reason I won the **Most Valuable Camper** trophy. Helping others, not quitting, and putting up with Anna without getting mad helped too.

Nick behaved himself on the bus going home. He thought the bus driver would make him get off if he caused trouble. But when we got home, he told his mom I tried to drown him. Of course, she didn't believe it.

Jenny was still covered in pink lotion spots on the bus. She sat in the back and didn't try to take anyone's window seat. She was **almost nice** for a whole week.

Then she was mean old Jenny Pinski again.

Monica's parents were so proud of the silver  spurs they didn't make her wait to take riding lessons. Now she rides one Saturday a month.

Becca was just glad her camping days were over forever.

About two weeks after we got back, my mom told me I had a letter. It was from Blue River Camp. **I was nervous while I opened the envelope.**

Dear Claudia,

We're thrilled to let you know that you've been chosen to be a junior counselor at Blue River Camp next summer! All of the counselors and instructors are excited to have you here next year.

Congratulations!

Claudia's Camp Survival Tips #18-#20:

Look on the bright side, do your best, and don't give up.

The End

About the Author

Diana G. Gallagher lives in Florida with her husband and five dogs, four cats, and a cranky parrot. Her hobbies are gardening, garage sales, and grandchildren. She has been an English equitation instructor, a professional folk musician, and an artist. However, she had aspirations to be a professional writer at the age of twelve. She has written dozens of books for kids and young adults.

About the Illustrator

Brann Garvey grew up in the great state of Iowa, where he studied art and visual communications. He graduated from the Minneapolis College of Art and Design with a degree in illustration. Brann is usually found with one or more of the following: a pencil in his hand, a comic book, a remote for watching DVDs, or his pet kitty, Iggy. When the weather is nice, Brann likes to play disc golf, and he proudly points out that Iowa is one of the world's centers for the sport. Iggy does not play.

Glossary

bridle (BRYE-duhl)—the straps that control a horse

corral (kuh-RAL)—a fenced area for horses

counselor (KOUN-suh-lur)—a person who supervises kids at camp

cramp (KRAMP)—pain caused by a muscle tightening

dog paddle (DOG PAD-uhl)—an easy way to swim by just moving your arms and kicking your feet

fungus (FUHN-guhss)—a type of plant that has no leaves, flowers, or roots. A mushroom is a kind of fungus.

intermediate (in-tur-MEE-dee-it)—in the middle, or in between two things. If someone is an intermediate swimmer, they are neither a beginner nor advanced.

klutz (KLUHTS)—a clumsy person

outhouse (OUT-houss)—an outdoor bathroom building

stroke (STROHK)—a method of swimming. Overhand, breast stroke, and backstroke are some of the different kinds of swimming strokes.

tread (TRED)—if you are treading water, you are swimming in one place with your body in a vertical position

Discussion Questions

1. There are some bullies in this story. Sometimes Anna bullies Claudia, and at camp, Jenny is bullied by Roberta. How do you deal with bullies? What are some things you can do when a bully is bothering you?

2. In this book, Claudia's goal is to become a junior counselor. What are some of the things she does to achieve that goal? What else could she have done? Did she do anything wrong? Talk about it.

3. What do you think is the hardest thing that Claudia had to do while she was at camp? Explain your answer.

Writing Prompts

1. Claudia and her friends do a lot while they're at camp! Which of their activities seems like the most fun to you? Pick one of the things that the kids at Claudia's camp do and write about it.

2. It can be interesting to think about a story from another person's point of view. Try writing the "Tip A Canoe" section (on page 62) from Anna's point of view. What does Anna think about while she and Claudia are out on the lake? What does she see? How does she feel?

3. At the end of this book, many of the campers receive awards. Make a list of your five closest friends. Think about how those friends have acted over the last week. Now make up a list of awards for your friends! If you're feeling extra creative, you can draw pictures of the awards too.

MORE FUN
with Claudia!

DANCE TRAP

THE COMPLICATED LIFE OF
Claudia
Cristina
Cortez
BY DIANA G. GALLAGHER

STONE ARCH Realistic Fiction

GUILTY!
THE COMPLICATED LIFE OF
Claudia
Cristina
Cortez
BY DIANA G. GALLAGHER

STONE ARCH Realistic Fiction

THE COMPLICATED LIFE OF
Claudia
Cristina
Cortez
BY DIANA G. GALLAGHER

Claudia Cristina Cortez

Just like every other thirteen-year-old girl, Claudia
Cristina Cortez has a complicated life. Whether she's
studying for the big Quiz Show, babysitting her neighbor,
Nick, avoiding mean Jenny Pinski, planning the seventh-
grade dance, or trying desperately to pass the swimming
test at camp, Claudia goes through her complicated life
with confidence, cleverness, and a serious dash of cool.

WHATEVER
JOURNAL

Internet Sites

Do you want to know more about subjects related to this book? Or are you interested in learning about other topics? Then check out FactHound, a fun, easy way to find Internet sites.

Our investigative staff has already sniffed out great sites for you!

Here's how to use FactHound:

1. Visit *www.facthound.com*

2. Select your grade level.

3. To learn more about subjects related to this book, type in the book's ISBN number: **159889840X**.

4. Click the **Fetch It** button.

FactHound will fetch the best Internet sites for you!